IF I FOUND A
WISTFUL UNICORN

to Martin

PUBLISHED BY
Peachtree Publishers, Ltd.
494 Armour Circle, N.E.
Atlanta, Georgia 30324

Text © 1978 Ann Ashford
Illustrations © 1978 Wilfred H. Drath

20 19 18 17 16

Manufactured in Mexico

ISBN 0-931948-00-2

Library of Congress Catalog Card Number 78-59094

IF I FOUND A WISTFUL UNICORN

A GIFT OF LOVE

by Ann Ashford
illustrated by Bill Drath

PEACHTREE
PUBLISHERS

IF I FOUND A WISTFUL UNICORN
AND BROUGHT HIM TO YOU, ALL FORLORN···
WOULD YOU PET HIM ?

IF I TOOK AN EMPTY MIDNIGHT TRAIN

ACROSS THE COUNTRY IN THE RAIN...

WOULD YOU MEET ME ?

IF I PICKED A LITTLE FLOWER UP
AND PUT IT IN A PAPER CUP···

WOULD YOU SMELL IT ?

IF I FOUND A SECRET PLACE TO GO,

WITH YOU THE ONLY ONE TO KNOW ···
WOULD YOU BE THERE ?

IF MY CRICKET COUGHED AND GOT THE FLU

AND NEEDED WARMTH AND COMFORT TOO...

WOULD YOU HOLD HIM ?

IF MY RAINBOW WERE TO TURN ALL GRAY
AND WOULDN'T SHINE AT ALL TODAY ···

WOULD YOU PAINT IT ?

IF MY BIRCH TREE WERE AFRAID AT NIGHT
AND COULDN'T SLEEP WITHOUT A LIGHT···

WOULD YOU BRING ONE ?

IF MY SOUL WERE FEELING ALL ALONE
AND WASN'T NEAR A TELEPHONE...

WOULD YOU WRITE TO IT ?

IF MY CLOCK DEVELOPED NERVOUS STRAIN

AND NEEDED HELP TO "TOCK" AGAIN ...

WOULD YOU FIX IT ?

IF I RAN BACKWARDS UP A TREE

AND CALLED FOR YOU TO

IF MY TURTLE GOT A NERVOUS TIC
AND COULDN'T SWIM 'CAUSE HE WAS SICK···

WOULD YOU SIT WITH HIM ?

IF I SAID THAT I COULD DANCE FOR YOU
AS HARD AS THAT WOULD BE TO DO···

WOULD YOU WATCH ME ?

IF MY PET TURNIP TURNED ON ME

AND BIT ME FIERCELY ON THE KNEE ...

WOULD YOU BANDAGE IT ?

IF MY OBELISK CAME TUMBLING DOWN
AND FELL IN PIECES ON THE GROUND...

WOULD YOU PICK IT UP ?

IF MY NIGHTINGALE WERE A MONOTONE

AND MUCH TOO SHY TO SING ALONE...

WOULD YOU HUM WITH HIM ?

IF MY WART DECIDED YESTERDAY

TO BE A DIMPLE ANYWAY ...

WOULD YOU NOTICE ?

IF ALL THAT I WOULD WANT TO DO

WOULD BE TO SIT AND TALK TO YOU ...

WOULD YOU LISTEN ?

IF ANY OF THESE THINGS YOU'LL DO,

I'LL NEVER HAVE SAY TO YOU...

"DO YOU LOVE ME ?"

S imple yet profound, *If I Found A Wistful Unicorn* has touched the lives of thousands of people and continues to make new friends wherever it goes. Here are a few comments from the many letters we have received since this special book was published in 1978:

"I found such richness in…your marvelously profound, elegant little book. I really appreciate your sharing this unique gift and insight with us—in such an understandable way."

—W.K., Dallas, TX

"I bought a copy of the book If I Found a Wistful Unicorn *while vacationing in Georgia a few years back. Today I have met someone I care for very much and I would also like to share this book with him…. This book is one of my most treasured keepsakes."*

—S.G., Coal Run, Ohio

"I was touched by its beauty, simplicity and love. It is truly a wonderful book and expresses feelings I have had and still do regarding love and closeness. I just wanted you to know that your book has touched the heart of someone and to thank you for your work."

—K.K., West Lafayette, IN

"I never thought I'd fall in love again. Your book is a treasure."

—J.S., Florence, AL

"I don't usually write but felt so inclined because of the warmth and real feeling the both of you offered in your work…. God bless the both of you wonderful and sensitive people."

—B.W., Irving, TX

"I do not find the proper English words to tell you how deeply this masterpiece has touched my heart. I really, platonically, love your soul, for having written this poem which says in such a delicate, subtle, feminine way all the dreams of a man, all his hopes, his foolish hopes, his childish hopes, his desperate need for understanding, for affection, for tenderness, for love."

—A.N., Lausanne, Switzerland

"I found it rather remarkable. It seems at first a little light confection, nice and pretty—but days after it has been put aside it floats back into your consciousness a bit like a whiff of perfume after the young lady has already passed."

—K.Q., Atlanta, GA